7/95

Bertha's Garden

Written by Elisabeth Dyjak

Illustrated by Janet Wilkins

Houghton Mifflin Company
Boston 1995

Library of Congress Cataloging-in-Publication Data

Dyjak, Elisabeth.
Bertha's garden / by Elisabeth Dyjak ; illustrated by Janet
Wilkins.
p.   cm.
Summary: As Mr. Rabbit enjoys sampling the vegetables in Bertha's
garden, she becomes increasingly angry and plans to get even with
him.
ISBN 0-395-68715-2
[1. Gardens—Fiction.   2. Rabbits—Fiction.]   I. Wilkins, Janet,
ill.   II. Title.
PZ7.D9894Be   1995   93-28594
[E]—dc20   CIP
                           AC

Printed in Hong Kong

DNH   10   9   8   7   6   5   4   3   2   1

For Eleanor,
　　gardener of gardeners,
And James,
　　bearer of roses.

Sunday morning. Mr. Rabbit in his thicket.
Munch munch. "Ho-hum, dandelions."

hop, hop, hippity hop

wiggle nose
sniff sniff

Cautiously is the way Mr. Rabbit
approaches Bertha's garden.

"A little corner of heaven!
All my favorites, Bertha planted just for me!"

nibble nibble, spit out beetle
"That Bertha is one fine lady!"

Sunny Monday.

hop, hippity hop

wiggle nose
sniff sniff

"I do declare! Look at those flip-flappers
flip-flapping up in the air!"

flippity flippity flap
spin and leap

shuffle to the cabbage,
slide to the carrots

kick a rotting rutabaga
"Ugh! Rutabagas give me big bellyache."

Rainy Tuesday.
pitter patter

hop, hop
sniff

"Why, twitch my ears, untangle my toes!
What do I hear?"

tinkle tinkle clink
tinkle tinkle clang

pitter patter pitter patter
Pluck a pea. Pluck a pea.
"Yummy!"

Wednesday evening.
Oh, so quiet.

hop
sniff

"I'll be—Bertha sent me company."
yakety yakety yak yakety yum yum

STOMP STOMP STOMP
Bertha shakes.
Earth quakes.
"That rabbit brings out
the worst in me!"

Moonlit Thursday.

hop, hop

Please do NOT
eat the
lettuce.
Bertha

Mr. Rabbit gropes in pocket, past yesterday's radish top.
Finds pencil at the bottom next to sticky old gumdrop.

A, B, C,
D—Duck dumplings, E—Eggy fooey yong, F—Fudge,
G, H, I, J, K, L, M, N, O, P,
Q—Quail delight, R—Rabbit . . .

"Hmm." Bertha is inspired.

Friday dawn.
hop

"This sign business is fun!"
With a careful paw he writes,

"A family favorite, a never-fail dish," Bertha growls.
"Roll the little scoundrel in flour, brown in fat."

Clanging through kettles, spooning out lard.
"Humph! Hop, hop, hippity hop in my POT!"

Saturday noon.
tinkle tinkle clink
tinkle tinkle clang

shuffle foot
stomp and slide

"Good afternoon, Bertha.
I brought you some posies. You like?"

"MY ROSES!" Bertha roars.
"The last of my American Sweethearts!"

"MY SCARECROW!"
Mr. Rabbit smiles.

"So nice of you to send me company.

Say, thank you for the bow tie.
A handsome shade of pink,
don't you think?

Oh, how I love pie plate music!"

sniff
"What's for lunch?"

"Lunch? Is the fuzzy little bunny
fond of rutabagas in a *very* special stew?"

LE—AP!

"Ah . . . ah . . . rutabagas . . .
give me big bellyache.
Excuse me, dear Ber——"

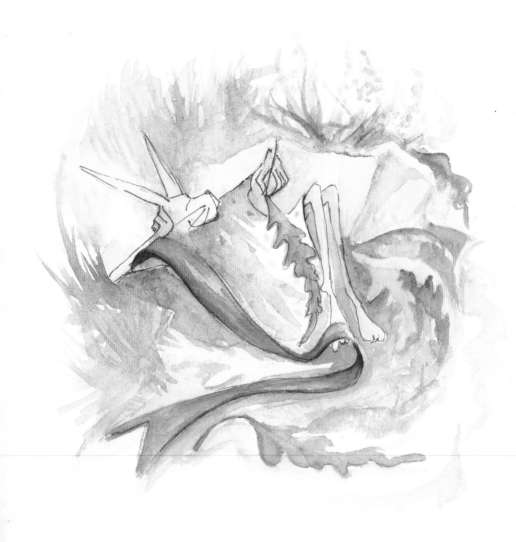

Mr. Rabbit back in his thicket.
Munch munch. "Yum, yum, dandelions!"